PEOPLE UNDERGROUND

Nicolas Brasch

NELSON CENGAGE Learning™

Australia • Brazil • Japan • Korea • Mexico • Singapore • Spain • United Kingdom • United States

People Underground

Fast Forward
Purple Level 19

Text: Nicolas Brasch
Editor: Cameron Macintosh
Designer: Vonda Pestana
Series designer: James Lowe
Production controller: Seona Galbally
Photo research: Gillian Cardinal
Audio recordings: Juliet Hill, Picture Start
Spoken by: Matthew King and Abbe Holmes
Reprint: Jennifer Foo

Acknowledgements
The author and publisher would like to acknowledge permission to reproduce material form the following sources: Photographs by Corbis Australia, pp. 18, 21/ Eric Pasquler, p. 19/ Paul A. Souders, pp. 23, 23; Getty Images/ James G. Welgos/ Stringer, p. 6/ Photographers Choice/ Kim Westerskov, p. 15/ Photonica/ Henrik Sorensen, front cover/ Stone/ Dave Saunders, p. 8/ Stone/ David Hiser, p. 11/ Stone/ John & Eliza Forder, p. 12/ Taxi/ Greg Pease, p. 9; Oliver Bolch, p. 20; Photolibrary/ A.G.E. Fotostock/ David A. Dobbs, p. 7/ Index Stock Imagery/ Alessandro Gandolfi, p. 3/ Index Stock Imagery/ Alessandro Gandolfi, p. 17/ Index Stock Imagery/ Bill Bachmann, p. 4/ John Fairfax Publications Pty Limited, p. 10/ Oxford Scientific Press/ Mark Webster, back cover, p. 13/ Peter Arnold/ Klas Andrews, p. 5/ Photo Researchers, Inc./ F. Stuart Westmorland, p. 14/ Robin Smith, p. 16.

ISBN 978 0 17 012654 0
ISBN 978 0 17 012645 8 (set)

Cengage Learning Australia
Level 7, 80 Dorcas Street
South Melbourne, Victoria Australia 3205
Phone: 1300 790 853

Cengage Learning New Zealand
Unit 4B Rosedale Office Park
331 Rosedale Road, Albany, North Shore NZ 0632
Phone: 0800 449 725

For learning solutions, visit **cengage.com.au**

Printed in Australia by Ligare Pty Ltd
6 7 8 9 10 11 12 21 20 19 18 17

THE UNIVERSITY OF MELBOURNE

Evaluated in independent research by staff from the Department of Language, Literacy and Arts Education at the University of Melbourne.

PEOPLE UNDERGROUND

Nicolas Brasch

Contents

Chapter 1	Under the Ground	4
Chapter 2	Working Underground	6
Chapter 3	Playing Underground	12
Chapter 4	Living Underground	16
Glossary and Index		24

Chapter 1

UNDER THE GROUND

As people walk around,
they take in the sights and the sounds around them.
They take notice of what other people are doing
and how they are acting.
They also take notice of other people working and playing,
and of the homes that they live in.

But people rarely take time to think about what is going on under their feet. A lot goes on under the surface of the Earth, and much of it involves people working, playing and even sleeping.

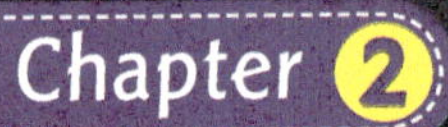

WORKING UNDERGROUND

Coal mining is one of the main work-related activities that occurs underground.
People have worked underground mining coal since the 1800s.

Coal mining became an industry in the 1800s because of the **Industrial Revolution**.
During the Industrial Revolution, large factories were built to produce many kinds of goods.

Coal is a source of energy.
In the 1800s, it provided fuel for machinery in factories and for steam trains that transported the goods.
It was also used to heat houses.

Running Words 162

Coal is still mined today.
While some of the machinery and equipment used to collect and transport coal is different from that used in the 1800s, coal mining still requires people to work underground.

Coal miners who work underground have four main tasks.
First, they operate equipment that makes tunnels underground.
These tunnels give miners access to the coal.
They also allow miners to walk or crawl through the mine.
Tracks are laid in the tunnels so that carts and other vehicles can transport coal and people.

Second, coal miners operate equipment that keeps tunnels from collapsing. For example, coal miners use bolting machines to drill holes in the mine roof to insert bolts that support the roof.

Third, coal miners operate equipment
that drills through the ground and collects the coal.
The coal is then transported to the surface.
Transporting the coal is the fourth main
underground task of coal miners.

Chapter 3

PLAYING UNDERGROUND

People have found ways of using areas underground for recreation. Caving is one of the most popular underground recreations. It involves finding and exploring caves.

Some caves that cavers explore are in the earth. Cavers access these caves by climbing into them. Other caves that cavers explore are underwater. Cavers access underwater caves by diving underwater and finding a hole into the cave.

Cavers who explore underwater caves have to use special diving equipment. They need to have done a lot of diving before they try to explore underwater caves.

Exploring underground and underwater caves is a dangerous but exciting recreation.

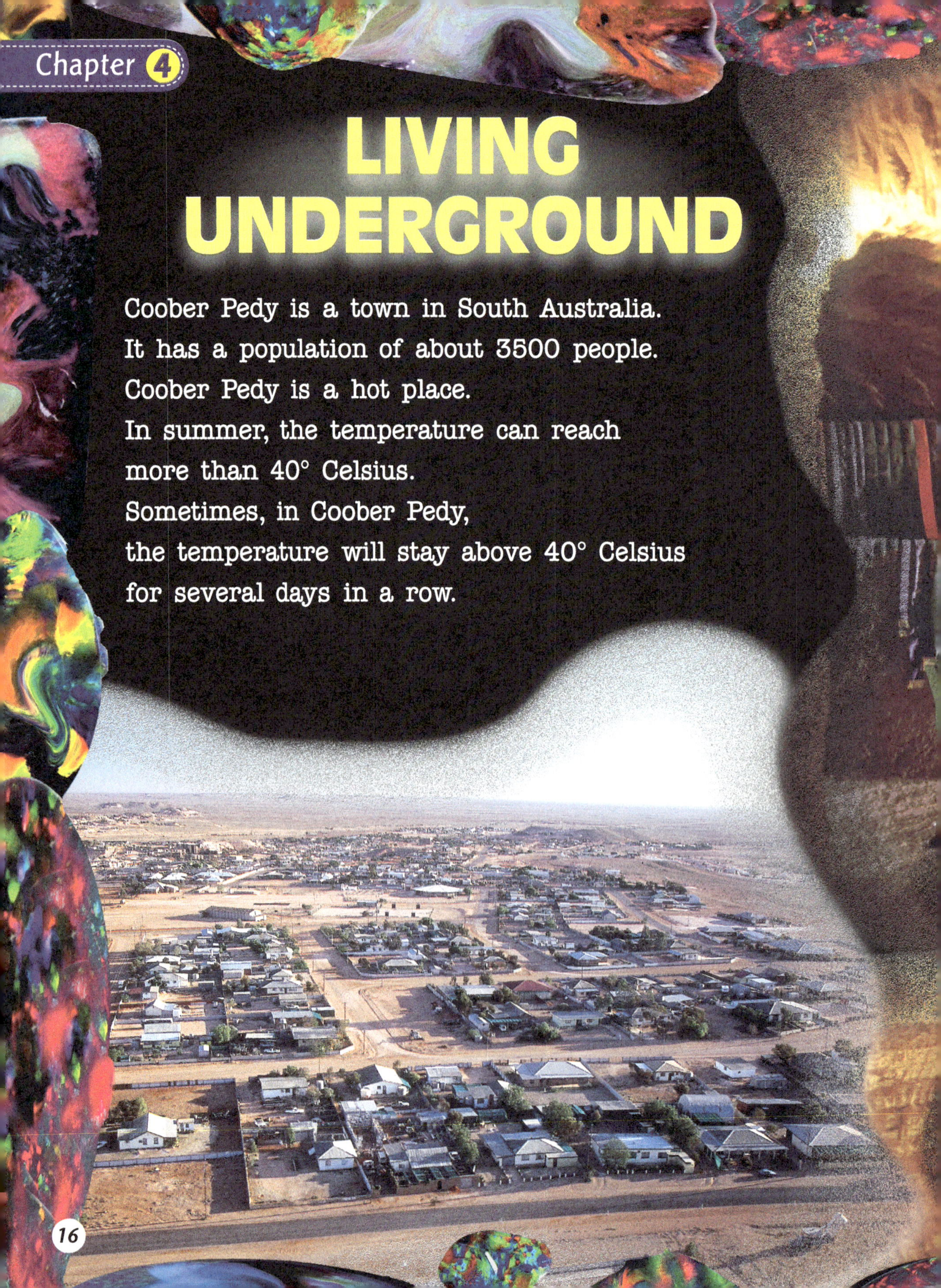

Chapter 4

LIVING UNDERGROUND

Coober Pedy is a town in South Australia.
It has a population of about 3500 people.
Coober Pedy is a hot place.
In summer, the temperature can reach more than 40° Celsius.
Sometimes, in Coober Pedy, the temperature will stay above 40° Celsius for several days in a row.

Because Coober Pedy is such a hot place, most people who live there live underground.

Living underground may seem like a strange way to live, but it works well for the people of Coober Pedy because it is so hot there.

The name Coober Pedy is believed to come from the Aboriginal words "kupa" and "piti", which together mean "white man in a hole".

In Coober Pedy, there are underground houses, hotels and shops.
There is even an underground church, an underground art gallery and underground museums.

Most underground homes are built in old mines. People get natural light through holes cut into the earth. The holes have glass panes put over them that let the sunlight in but keep dirt and other materials out.

The people of Coober Pedy also get their water from underground.
Their water comes to them through a pipeline from an underground water source about 25 kilometres from the town.

People choose to live in Coober Pedy
because it is close to
most of the world's supply of opals.
Coober Pedy is known as the
"Opal Capital of the World".

Opal was first found in Coober Pedy
on 1 February 1915.
Since then, this small town
has been supplying the world with beautiful opals.

Glossary

Industrial Revolution a time, mainly in the 1800s, when goods were first produced in factories on a large scale

Index

caving 12–15
coal 6-11
coal mining 6, 8–11
Coober Pedy 16–23
equipment 8, 10, 11, 14
Industrial Revolution 6
miners 9, 10–11
opals 22–23
recreation 12, 15
underwater caves 13, 14–15